THE CATNAPPING CAPER

The Catnapping Caper

Mary Anderson

Illustrated by Blanche Sims

A Yearling Book

Published by
Dell Publishing
a division of
Bantam Doubleday Dell Publishing Group, Inc.
666 Fifth Avenue
New York, New York 10103

ISBN: 0-440-40236-0

Printed in the United States of America

November 1989

10 9 8 7 6 5 4 3 2 1

CWO

THE CATNAPPING CAPER.

THE FALTERING GREEK

1

"What's the matter with you?" Katie asked her brother. "Are you crazy or what? Why don't you want to see Melvin the Talking Cat? He's the most famous animal in the country. In the *world*, maybe!"

Hector poked at his cereal. "I'm busy, that's why," he said.

Katie smelled a rat. Her younger brother had never passed up a freebie in his life. Mom and Dad were paying for the tickets to the cat show, so Hector's cheapness wasn't the reason.

Something must be up.

"Busy?" she asked, suspiciously. "Doing

1

what? Since Ben and I made you a full-fledged member of R.I.S.K., it's your executive duty to come to the cat show."

Katie wasn't thrilled that her brother was a member of the cat club she'd started. True, he'd thought up the name ... Rescuers In Search of Kitties ... but he wasn't serious about it, like her best friend, Ben.

Katie and Ben loved cats and wanted to find good homes for all strays. So far, their success had made them both cat experts. In fact, Katie hoped to become a vet when she grew up. Or maybe even an animal psychiatrist. After all, cats had emotional problems, too.

Over the past few months, Katie and Ben had made several kids at school new members of R.I.S.K. Even Hector had dredged up some sappy little friends who wanted to join. But the important executive business of the club was still handled by herself and Ben. That suited Katie fine. After all, her brother knew he'd only been made an executive member under their parents' pressure.

Was that why he never took club business seriously? No, Katie decided; it was greed, pure and simple. With Hector, when money was involved, everything else went out the window. So at the moment, she was dying to discover what her sneaky brother was hiding.

"What's up? A hot baseball game?"

"No," he explained. "A job. Miss Barclay wants me to cat-sit with her Siamese this weekend. She's going out of town and needs someone to watch Sebastian."

"I knew it must have something to do with *money*."

Katie thought it unfair that Hector had turned their cat rescue operation into a money-making proposition. They were supposed to *save* cats, not get paid to sit with them. Hector had been typically greedy, using the club to set up his own business. He charged two dollars a day for cat-sitting and already had several clients.

"We're supposed to be a *charitable* organization," she scolded. "Maybe Ben and I will vote you out of the club."

"You can't," he said, smugly. "You *have* to keep me. Mom and Dad said so. After all the sneaky, dirty tricks you and Ben played on me—"

"Okay, okay. Stay home and make two dollars. See if I care."

"Four," Hector corrected. "Per day. Miss Barclay doubled my usual rate. Sebastian is a

3

valuable cat and needs special attention. Special medicines, too. He gets pink pills with breakfast and green pills with lunch. And smelly drops at night."

"Sebastian is a hypochondriac. He should eat less and get some therapy."

Hector looked uneasy, afraid Katie might horn in on his operation. Usually, it only took him a few minutes to feed his cats and change their litter. Easy money. Except for Sebastian, of course. He was different and needed extra attention. And lots of company. But Hector didn't mind. Miss Barclay let him eat all he liked and watch TV.

"You leave fat old Sebastian alone," he warned. "He's *my* client."

"I'm not interested in pampered pets," Katie said haughtily. "Hungry, homeless cats are supposed to be our business. And now, just because you won't come along to the cat show, some poor kitties may *starve*."

Hector nearly choked on his cereal. "How do you figure that?"

"The free samples, little brother. They give out tons of them each year. Ben and I had it all figured out. With three of us on line, we could get more food for our strays."

5

"Sorry," said Hector, unmoved. "I've got work to do. Business first."

Katie frowned. Hector wasn't only greedy. He was heartless, too.

2

At noon, Katie met her friend, Ben, outside their apartment building. As they sat on the bus on their way to the cat show, she explained why Hector hadn't come.

"Typical," said Ben, sympathetically. "Your brother sure loves money."

"He's sneaky, too," said Katie. "I know Miss Barclay only hired him because he's in our cat club. She thinks he's nuts about animals. Little does she know."

Ben agreed. "Yeah, I bet Hector is sitting over at her house right now, eating her food and reading her magazines."

"It's a good thing we wore our sneakers," said Katie. "Now we'll have to wait on those free sample lines twice as long. I hope we have time to meet Melvin."

The Imperial Cat Show was a yearly affair, and the children really looked forward to it. Breeders from all over the country brought their cats for display, hoping they'd win prizes. Free samples of the latest dry foods, canned foods and moist cat foods were given away by manufacturers.

But it wasn't just the free samples that interested Ben and Katie. There were lots of brochures filled with helpful information about the care and maintenance of cats. They faithfully collected every pamphlet to add to their Cat Care File.

Often, when Katie and Ben were supposed to be doing their homework together, they'd make plans for their future, instead. Some day, they wanted to open a joint veterinary practice and help hundreds of animals.

Attending the cat show was always fun, too. Each year, a different celebrity cat would make a special guest appearance. This year, the most famous cat of all was to be there: Melvin, The Talking Cat.

Melvin had achieved almost overnight fame as the spokesman for Meow Chow on television. His commercials were seen around the world. There was even talk of starring Melvin in a movie.

Melvin, a large white shorthair with a lustrous coat and bright blue eyes, was a unique animal. A born ham, he loved to perform for the camera. But his chief claim to fame was a series of distinct meows that sounded just like real words. Fans across the country looked forward to Melvin's commercials. Many swore they could actually hear him say "Meow Chow."

Naturally, the owners of The Meow Chow Company were thrilled with Melvin. There was a rumor he had a multimillion-dollar lifetime contract. In addition to his TV stardom, Melvin also had tons of related products on the market. There were Melvin shirts, Melvin stuffed toys, Melvin calendars, Melvin games, plus Melvin sheets, pillowcases and pajamas. Katie and Ben could hardly wait to meet him in person.

"You think he'll be wearing sunglasses?" Ben joked.

Arriving at the arena, the children paid for

their tickets at the front window. Then a guard directed them up the stairs toward a gold and blue banner, which announced that The Imperial Cat Show was in progress.

As the crowds hurried through the doors, Katie and Ben were once again reminded of how many cat lovers there were in town.

"I wish we could get all their names and addresses," said Katie. "We could put them in our Potential Owner File."

"That's a neat idea," said Ben. "Maybe next year we could rent a booth here and pass out information about R.I.S.K. I bet lots of these folks would like a cute little stray cat."

Katie wasn't sure. "I'll bet they're all interested in pedigrees."

"Melvin has no pedigree," Ben noted. "I read he was an ordinary housecat before he became a star. His trainer bought him from some guy for almost nothing."

Katie remembered reading that article in the newspaper, too. Victor Henderson, Melvin's owner and trainer, had bought the cat four years earlier for a mere ten dollars. He realized the cat's unique talents could earn a fortune. Melvin's original owner, Barney Carter, was now furious with Henderson.

"You're right," Katie agreed. "Melvin *was* a typical cat before he became famous. So maybe one of the strays we rescue from the street will be a star someday, too."

Once inside the cat show, the children were torn between duty and pleasure. What should they do first? View the various cats competing for awards? Meet Melvin? Or stand on long lines collecting free samples? Practicality and duty won out.

"We'll get our orphans their food first," said Katie.

She and Ben had always thought cat lovers were special individuals. "Guess when it comes to free samples, they turn into nuts, like everybody else."

Long lines of people were pushing and shoving for their free packets of kitty deodorant, kitty litter and kitty food. The workers in the booths kept shoving out little plastic bags full of things, in a frantic effort to meet the demand.

Katie observed one fat woman return to the Nibbly Noshes line four times, until her arms were too full to carry any more.

"My cat, Benjamin, just loves Nibbly Noshes," she confessed, slightly embarrassed.

11

Ben was willing to bet her cat was twice as fat as she was!

After an hour of standing, waiting, shoving and collecting, Katie and Ben had amassed four shopping bags filled with everything from protein-enriched pellets to cat candies. When they returned home, it would all go into their future food supply for future strays.

Now it was time for fun. They hurried to the center arena, where Melvin was proudly greeting his many fans. Unfortunately, the line to meet him was longer than all the others. Putting down their shopping bags, they leaned over, hoping to catch a glimpse of the famous star. But there were dozens of people ahead of them.

"There he is," Katie shouted, pointing down the line. "He's sitting on a fancy wooden pedestal. On a velvet pillow, I think."

Melvin was a real professional. He didn't seem put off by the crowds surrounding him. In fact, he was enjoying the attention. On the table beside him was a large stack of his newly published book, *From the Mouth of Melvin*. This was a collection of cat jokes and witticisms, which Melvin was personally pawgraphing for his fans. For those willing to pay $9.95,

Melvin's trainer, a burly, balding man, placed the cat's paw on a stamp pad. This created an original Melvin pawgraph. Lots of people were happily buying the book.

Waiting to meet Melvin, Katie counted the people in line ahead of her. There were twenty. As things moved along, they were soon up to number ten.

But then Victor Henderson made an announcement.

"Sorry folks, it's Melvin's lunch break. He'll be back in twenty minutes, ready to meet the rest of his fans."

Mr. Henderson placed the cat in his carrier, then led him through an exit door.

The children, not wanting to lose their place in line, decided to wait.

"I wonder what Melvin eats for lunch," Ben mused.

"I'll bet it's caviar," said Katie. "He certainly can afford it."

An exotic-looking foreign gentleman, standing in line ahead of the children, turned and smiled in agreement.

"Ah yes," he said, "this Melvin is a cat of great worth." Extending a gloved hand, he introduced himself. "My name is Omar. Long

ago in my country, Egypt, such cats were worshipped."

"Really?" asked Katie. "You mean like gods?"

"Indeed," Omar replied. "Statues of the cat-headed god, Bast, were most prized. In hieroglyphics, there were five symbols for the cat. In fact, the word 'cat' in Egyptian is 'mau,' which also means sun. The sun god, Ra, was often seen in the form of a giant cat."

"Wow," said Ben. "I guess those ancient Egyptians liked cats even more than we do!"

Omar nodded knowingly. "Ah, so you are true cat lovers, also? I sensed this immediately. I imagine you have many felines of your own."

Ben thought it funny to consider the skinny strays they rescued from the streets "felines." None of them seemed fancy enough for such a term.

"We have no cats," Katie explained. "We can't. Ben's dad is allergic to them. And my dog, Scruffy, hates them. So we don't own any, even though we'd love to."

Omar seemed sympathetic. "A most sad situation. Often in life, we cannot have all that we wish, is that not so? I myself would dearly love to have an animal of such great value as Melvin."

"You mean you'd like to buy him?" asked Katie.

A strange expression appeared on the Egyptian man's face. "To buy such a feline would not be possible. And yet, to someday have such a cat . . . no, I must not talk of it. But since you are true cat fanciers, perhaps you would someday care to view my personal collection." Taking two cards from his pocket, he handed one each to the children. "I would be most honored to show them to you." Then bowing, he excused himself. "I must leave now."

"Wait," called Ben. "Aren't you going to stay and see Melvin?"

Omar looked strangely mysterious. "Oh, I shall see him, never fear."

Then he disappeared into the crowd.

"What a strange man," Katie noted, placing his card in her pocket. "I wonder what he meant by his collection. Isn't that a strange thing to call your pets?"

"Yeah," Ben agreed. "And I wonder why he left so suddenly."

Katie checked the large wall clock overhead.

She hoped Melvin's lunch break would soon be over. Another ten minutes to go.

Two people, tired of waiting for Melvin's return, suddenly dropped out of line.

"Look at that guy who just left," said Ben. "I know him from someplace. Is he an old teacher of ours? I never recognize them outside school. I've always gotta see them behind a desk."

"He's not a teacher," said Katie. She recognized the man's face from the newspaper. "That's Barney Carter, Melvin's original owner. I wouldn't think he'd have to wait on line to see his own cat. *Former* cat, I mean. Anyway, he looks real angry."

The children watched as Mr. Carter pushed his way out of line and hurried through the exit door.

"Guess you'd be angry, too," said Ben, "if you missed out on a fortune. Carter doesn't get one cent of Melvin's profits. It sure was a dumb idea for him to sell that cat. If I was him, I'd be dying to get him back."

"I'm just dying to *see* him," said Katie, impatiently.

After several more minutes, Victor Henderson reappeared. But he didn't have Melvin's

17

carrying case with him. Instead, he carried a piece of notepaper in his hand. Flashing it around, he shouted hysterically.

"This is terrible. Help me, someone. Melvin has been stolen!"

3

Catnapped! There was no doubt about it.

Poor Mr. Henderson was so distraught, it took several people to calm him down.

Within minutes, the arena's security guards were called into action. They tried to find out more details. But all Mr. Henderson could do was wave the note in front of their faces. The threatening words were scrawled out in purple marker:

I'VE TAKEN MELVIN. IF YOU WANT HIM BACK ALIVE, COME UP WITH A MILLION BUCKS. YOU WILL BE TOLD WHERE

TO BRING THE MONEY. BUT COME
ALONE. ANY SLIP-UPS AND MELVIN IS
A GONER.

Despite the protests of many of the people
at the cat show, the guards closed all the exits
until the police arrived.

"Sorry, folks, but no one leaves just yet. The
cops will have to investigate this business."

Most of the visitors took the matter in stride.
Several of the cat-judging contests proceeded,
as if nothing had happened. But Katie and
Ben were too upset to continue touring the
show. Naturally, they weren't half as upset as
Mr. Henderson. But they sympathized with
his problem. It must be terrible to have your
pet stolen, especially one as priceless as Melvin.

Katie tried to console the poor man. "Don't
worry, I'm sure the police will find Melvin."

"Yeah," added Ben. "Maybe it's all just a
horrible joke. No one would do anything mean
to Melvin."

Once Mr. Henderson's initial hysteria was
over, he seemed dazed. The children helped
him to a chair.

"I can't understand how it happened," he
mumbled. "Melvin . . . gone. I can't believe it.

20

I only left him for a couple of minutes. He'd just finished his food, so I let him rest in his carrier while I went out to grab a cigarette. I was only in the hall for one smoke. When I got back, he was gone. There was nothing . . . except this lousy note."

Katie glanced at the note again. "At least it's a clue. I bet the police can figure out a lot from this."

"What's to figure?" shouted Mr. Henderson. "Some creep wants a million bucks in exchange for Melvin."

"Well," said Katie, "at least you're lucky to be able to pay the ransom."

Victor Henderson looked at her as if she were crazy. "Pay it? *I* can't pay it! Who's got a million bucks?"

Ben figured Melvin must be worth five times that much, and said so.

Mr. Henderson shook his head. "I know you kids are trying to help, but you don't understand. Sure, I'm Melvin's owner and trainer, but most of his dough is in investments. These crooks want cash—hard cash—understand? And I don't have it."

"Don't worry," said Katie. "The police will find Melvin, you'll see."

21

Within half an hour, the police were on the scene. After questioning Mr. Henderson, they proceeded to make a thorough search of the area. They began by examining the back room where Melvin was last seen.

Chief of detectives David McCullough was in charge.

"Dust everything for fingerprints," he instructed his patrolmen. "If we're lucky, we'll find some clues."

Unfortunately, none turned up. The room was clean as a whistle.

"Whoever took your cat," explained the detective, "probably wore gloves."

Katie and Ben stood to one side, fascinated by the investigation. It wasn't every day they got to see real detectives at work.

"Gosh, Hector would love this," whispered Katie.

Her brother, a crime comic freak, was going to be green with envy when he found out what he'd missed by not coming to the cat show. Well, it served him right. Maybe Hector didn't care about Melvin, but he sure would be angry when he discovered he could have met real "crimebusters."

"Shouldn't you call in the F.B.I.?" asked

Ben. "Aren't they supposed to handle kidnappings?"

Detective McCullough smiled. "That's true, son. But this is a *cat*napping. I don't think the federal government will get involved."

Katie thought that was unfair. Perhaps in the future, R.I.S.K. could do something about getting equal rights for cats.

"Our best bet is to question all the exhibitors," said the detective. "Maybe someone saw something."

"Can we tag along?" asked Katie. "We're true cat lovers and want to help."

McCullough glanced at Mr. Henderson. "Is that okay with you?"

"I don't care." He sighed. "I suppose we need all the help we can get."

"All right, kids, but don't get in the way."

Katie and Ben piled their shopping bags in a corner, then followed the detective into the center arena. There, he systematically examined all the cages, hoping Melvin might be hidden inside one.

They checked through all the Siamese, Maltese, Manx and Persians. They examined the Russian Blues, Calicos, Burmese and Balinese. The Cornish Rex and the Himalayan. And of

course, all the house cats, too. Especially the white ones.

Lots of the cats were sleeping on fancy blanketed beds or playing with toys their owners had placed in their cages. Many of the owners didn't appreciate having their cherished animals awakened from their catnaps. But Detective McCullough was determined to leave no cat unturned!

"Sorry," he kept saying, "you'll have to hold your cat up for inspection."

Ben thought the whole procedure slightly amusing. Sort of like a cat line-up.

After an hour, Victor Henderson sadly informed the police that none of the cats was his famous Melvin. The thorough search was complete. The police now determined that Melvin had definitely been removed from the area.

"Well," said the detective, "I guess there's no point in holding all these people any longer. Whoever wants to leave is allowed to go. We'll take this note over to the lab for testing. In the meantime, I suggest you start making plans to pay the ransom."

"A million bucks!" groaned Mr. Henderson. "Where am I gonna get the money!"

4

That evening, as was the custom in the Morrison household, Katie's parents asked their children all about the events of their day.

Hector, looking disgustingly self-satisfied, began.

"I made four dollars. I watched three movies. And I ate a box of chocolates."

Mrs. Morrison frowned. "Hector, you didn't."

"Miss Barclay said I could. She lets me have anything I want. She says I'm precious."

Katie thought she'd barf. She hadn't said a word about the catnapping yet. She was saving it for dinnertime, so she could see Hector squirm with envy.

27

Naturally, she was concerned about Melvin's theft, but she also wanted to get even with her brother.

"What happened at the cat show?" asked Mr. Morrison. "Did you and Ben have a good time?"

"Sure, it was great. We collected lots of free food for our strays. But something awful happened, too, Dad. Melvin The Talking Cat was *stolen*."

"That's awful," said Mrs. Morrison. "I watch Melvin on TV all the time. Who'd do such a thing?"

"The police don't know yet, Mom. Ben and I talked with the detective in charge of the case. In fact, we helped him with the investigation. The thief wants a million dollars!"

Katie's parents looked stunned. But it was nothing compared to the expression on Hector's face. He actually turned slightly green.

"Investigation?" he gasped. "Detectives? You mean I missed out on all that neat stuff? Why didn't you tell me?"

"I thought you weren't interested in cat shows," she said, coolly. "Detective McCullough said Ben and I were really helpful. We assisted with the interrogation. And we met Melvin's owner. There's a ransom note and everything."

Hector's green tint quickly turned to red. "You're a stinking rat, Katie! You have all the fun!"

"Hector, please," his father scolded. "There's nothing fun about this business. Do the police have any clues yet, Katie? Does this detective know who might've stolen Melvin?"

"Not yet. But I bet he will soon. I'm sure there's something about it on the news."

"Well let's watch," shouted Hector, hurrying from the table. Eagerly, he switched on the set.

Yes, there was definitely something about Melvin on the news. A blown-up photo of the famous cat was seen behind the newscaster as he explained all about the catnapping.

Detective McCullough was in the studio, as well as Victor Henderson and Hartley Reese, the president of Meow Chow. The children listened attentively as the detective explained things to the TV viewers. Then he announced that the police had just been ordered to cease their investigation of the case.

"What do you mean?" asked the reporter. "Aren't you going to find Melvin?"

"*I* asked the cops to drop the case," explained Henderson. "I don't want them involved in this deal. All I want is to get Melvin back, safe and sound."

"That's right," agreed Hartley Reese. "Melvin is a valued employee of my firm, Meow Chow. As its president, I've authorized my company to pay whatever ransom is demanded. I've also instructed the police to remove themselves from the case. Mr. Henderson and I plan to sit tight until we get further instructions from the catnapper. Money is no object. Melvin is priceless. We're willing to pay whatever we must in order to get him back."

The reporter was obviously surprised at this announcement. "Maybe the thief is out there watching right now. Is there anything you'd like to tell him, Mr. Henderson?"

"Yes, there is. Bring Melvin back to me, safe and sound, and there'll be no questions asked. I'm staying at the Camelot Hotel. I'll be there, waiting to hear from you. Mr. Reese promised to put up the money. Now all we want is for you to tell us where to leave it. In the meantime, take care of my cat. *Please.*"

"Well," concluded the reporter, "that was quite a heartwarming plea from Melvin's owner. If you're out there listening, Mr. Catnapper, all Melvin's fans across the country are hoping you don't hurt him. This is Walter Whitner, signing off."

Further on in the broadcast, a newswoman explained how she had tried to interview Barney Carter.

"Barney Carter, Melvin's former owner and proprietor of the barber shop here in town called The Clip Joint, was unavailable for comment today. He refused to talk to this reporter or anyone else."

Hearing that, Katie suddenly realized something. By the time Detective McCullough had arrived to search the arena, Barney Carter had left the cat show. Disappeared! Could it have been Carter who stole Melvin?

Then Katie remembered something else. McCullough had said that whoever stole Melvin had worn gloves. Omar, the strange Egyptian man, was wearing gloves. He, also, had mysteriously disappeared just before Melvin was stolen. Could he have been the thief?

Two suspects.

Two men, who both desperately wanted to own Melvin.

Two suspects the police knew nothing about.

Only she and Ben knew about them!

5

Later that night after Hector had gone to bed, Katie telephoned Ben.

"Did you watch the news?" she asked.

"I sure did. Funny, how the police dropped the case so fast. But I guess Mr. Henderson is real scared the thief might hurt Melvin."

"I suppose he's right. With the police snooping around, Melvin might be in danger. But if someone knew something important, they should do something about it, right?"

"What do you mean?"

"*Clues*, Ben. And leads. You and I are the only ones who know Barney Carter was at the cat show today."

"You think Carter nabbed Melvin?"

"Maybe. Or maybe that Egyptian man did it. He was wearing *gloves*, remember?"

"Yeah." Ben agreed. "And he acted peculiar. But what are you getting at, Katie?"

"I think we should investigate this crime ourselves. No one would suspect us, so Melvin wouldn't be in any danger."

"Say, that's a great idea. Where do we start?"

There was a moment's pause at Katie's end of the phone. Without her knowing it, Hector had tiptoed into the living room. He was listening in on their conversation.

"No one investigates anything without *me*," he threatened.

"Hey, Ben," whispered Katie. "You better get over here fast. We've got trouble."

Five minutes later, still in his pajamas, Ben had taken the elevator to Katie's apartment.

"What's up?" he asked, as she answered the door.

"Sshh," she cautioned. "Let's go into my room, so my folks can't hear."

Hector was seated on the bed, looking smugly immovable as Katie explained the situation.

"Fishface wants to be in on things, but I vote no."

"And I vote yes," said Hector. "This is a cat-related crime. As a senior member of R.I.S.K., I should be in on it."

"That means your vote is the deciding one. You don't want Hector tagging along with us, do you, Ben?"

"Before you answer that," said Hector, "keep in mind that I'm a blabbermouth. If you don't vote me in on this deal, I'll tell Mom and Dad everything. I don't think they'd like you chasing catnappers, now would they?"

"That's bribery," Ben shouted.

"I know it," he said, proudly. "But it's for your own good. After all, *I'm* the only one here who knows anything about criminals. You two may be experts on cats, but I'm an expert on crooks. Besides, finding Melvin will help my business."

"How do you figure that?" his sister asked. "Cat-*sitting* has nothing to do with cat*napping*."

"Publicity. The way I see it, whoever solves this crime is sure to wind up on the news. So when we crack this case, we'll be put on television. Then I can advertise my cat-sitting service, free of charge. I bet I'll get dozens of new customers."

Ben was disgusted. "What a slimy, low-down reason."

35

"I knew you'd like it. So what do you say?"

"Have we got a choice?"

"None. So tell me what you know so far, and we'll get started."

Against her better judgment, Katie filled her brother in on everything they knew about the catnapping. She explained all about Barney Carter and the strange exotic gentleman who wanted to own Melvin.

Hector listened attentively until she'd finished.

"Carter is too obvious a suspect," he concluded. "This guy Omar sounds like our man. And he's a foreigner, eh? That's suspicious right there. I say we track him down. Does he have a last name? There must be lots of Omars in the phone book."

"We don't need a phone book," said Katie. "We have his card." She ran to the chair where she'd left her jeans and took the calling card from her pocket.

It said: OMAR; DEALER IN ANIMAL RARITIES, with an address downtown.

"That settles it," said Hector. "We'll visit this guy tomorrow."

6

After breakfast, Hector could hardly wait to get started. But first, he had to bow out of a baseball game already arranged in the park. Then he made a fast trip over to Miss Barclay's apartment to feed Sebastian.

He waited impatiently as the cat finished off his food, the pink pill buried in the middle. He changed Sebastian's litter, then hurried home. There was no time to waste cat-sitting at the moment. The catnapping caper was far more important.

Going up in the elevator, Hector congratulated himself on how cleverly he'd wheedled his way into the whole investigation. So what if Katie and Ben didn't want him along? They never wanted him in on anything. Helping catch the crook who stole Melvin would mean a fortune for his business.

"What took you so long?" asked Katie when he returned.

"I'm a man of many responsibilities."

Katie sneered. "Well, just don't pull that dopey disguise business on us, okay? Last time we went snooping, you wanted us to wear *funny noses*. We're supposed to be inconspicuous."

"Really, Katie, that was *months* ago. I was only nine years old then! I know how to handle an investigation real good now."

"Excuse me! Look, Ben is waiting for us in the lobby. Let's get moving. I told Mom we're all going out together, so we're clear for the day. Just remember, if Omar is the thief, we don't want him to know we suspect him. He might do something awful and hurt Melvin. Sometimes, when kidnappers are afraid they'll be caught, they *kill* their victims."

Hector swore he'd be discreet. After all, a dead Melvin wouldn't be such hot advertising for his business!

They met Ben in the lobby, as arranged.

Then they all boarded the downtown bus. During the ride, Katie glanced at Omar's card.

"What do you suppose 'animal rarities' means?"

"I guess he owns a pet shop," said Ben.

"That's a *perfect* cover," said Hector. "Who'd think it was odd to see a cat in a pet shop? Yeah, we're on the right track, for sure."

Omar's address was in a downtown shopping area, a very exclusive part of town. There were several fancy jewelry stores, expensive dress shops and rare book emporiums.

"Real classy," Ben observed, "but a strange place for a pet shop."

Arriving outside the storefront, the children discovered it wasn't a pet shop after all. It was an arts and antiques gallery. A large bronze statue of a cat with a gold ring in its ear rested in the display window. Above the window, a brass-lettered sign announced: OMAR'S ANIMAL RARITIES.

Katie rang the bell. Presently, Omar answered. He looked much different from the day before at the cat show. He was wearing a long white cotton caftan and a funny little white cap on his head.

He seemed slightly surprised to see them.

39

Hector was very surprised to see Omar. Thinking the long white outfit was a night-gown, he apologized. "Sorry, I guess we woke you up, huh?"

"But of course not. Why should you think that?"

"Didn't you just get out of bed?"

Omar smiled as he glanced down at his clothes. "Ah, this garment. It is a costume of my native land. I find wearing it in the shop gives the surroundings a certain ambiance."

Hector didn't know what "ambiance" meant, but he was sure it was something suspicious. This Omar was definitely a sneaky guy. He looked like a character Hector had seen in an old horror movie, *The Mummy's Vengeance*. Those Egyptians were always putting curses on people or digging up dead things. Creepy!

Omar bowed politely. "So, my cat fanciers have come to visit."

"I brought my brother, too," said Katie.

"You are all most welcome. I'm sure you shall not be disappointed."

Hector wasn't fooled by the Egyptian's gracious manner. He knew lots of crooks were classy guys.

"I thought you had a pet shop," said Ben,

40

glancing around. "When you told us about your collection, I thought you meant cats."

"Ah, but they *are* cats. In a sense, my entire shop is a tribute to feline beauty. Naturally, none are alive."

Aha, thought Hector, just as he had suspected . . . *dead* things.

Proudly, Omar began giving the children a tour of his gallery. There were cat statuettes, cat portraits, and cat tapestries. Underneath glass cases rested a large collection of cat jewelry and cat china dishes. There were also cat lamps, pedestals in the shape of cats, engravings, golden charms, even some fancy gilded furniture with cat carvings.

A small stone sculpture caught Katie's attention.

"That's a sphinx, isn't it?"

"That's correct," said Omar. "A man with the body of a lion. This is but one indication of the reverence in which my people held all those of the cat family. It is a miniature replica of the Great Sphinx of Gizeh, which guards the Valley of the Nile."

Then Omar pointed to a statue by the far wall. "She is my most cherished possession." It was the figure of a woman with the head of

41

a cat. "She is the great goddess, Bastet, one of our most sacred animal gods."

Hector stared at the strange statue. "Say, how come you're such a cat crazy? I thought only Katie and Ben were cat freaks."

Omar smiled. "Perhaps because my ancient Egyptian ancestors bred what you now enjoy as the domestic house cat. Originally, they were small, wild cats of Africa."

"No kidding," said Ben, noticing a small object resting in the corner. It looked like a mummy case, but it, too, had the head of a cat. "What's that? Don't tell me Egyptians made *cats* into mummies."

"Indeed," explained Omar. "The great Pharaohs would often have cats entombed with their own mummified remains, for their journey into the afterlife. And sometimes cats were covered in precious jewels and placed in sacred cat cemeteries near the temple of the sacred city, Bubastis."

All this talk of mummies and cemeteries was giving Hector the creeps. By now, he was certain Omar had nabbed Melvin. After all, this guy was the world's greatest cat crazy, right? Naturally, he'd want to own the world's most famous cat.

While Omar continued to explain about cat

deities and the ancient cult of the cat, Hector decided to do some snooping on his own. He strolled around the gallery, pretending to be interested in all the objects. But he was actually interested in discovering a clue to Melvin's whereabouts. Maybe there was a secret panel or a neat trap door somewhere.

After several minutes of discreet investigation, Hector noticed something suspicious. There was a funny bump behind one of the large wall tapestries. Pushing the hanging aside slightly, he saw it was a shiny brass doorknob.

Wow, this was even better than a secret panel; it was a whole secret room!

Slowly, he began turning the knob.

"Stop!" shouted Omar, observing him from across the room.

Hector's hand froze against the doorknob.

The Egyptian's eyes flashed. "You mustn't go near there. Those objects are part of my private collection." Quickly regaining his composure, Omar smiled. "They are for select clients only," he explained. "No one can see them without a special appointment. I'm sure you understand."

"Yeah, sure," said Hector. A likely story, he thought. Hector knew exactly what was behind that door: it had whiskers and a tail!

Hurrying toward the wall, Omar quickly pulled the tapestry back in place, once again concealing the door. Then he walked over to a large glass case.

"I have some lovely scarabs in here. I'm sure you children would be interested in seeing them."

Katie nudged Hector. "What's up?"

"Something's hidden behind that secret door," he whispered. "And I bet it's Melvin!"

"Good work," said Ben. "We've gotta get in there and see."

"But how?" asked Katie. She glanced toward Omar, who was waiting to show them the scarabs. "We can't snoop while he's around. We've gotta get him out of here."

"Faint," whispered Ben.

Katie blinked. "Huh?"

"Not really. Just pretend. I'll handle the rest."

Katie had only seen people faint in the movies. With so many glass cases around, she was afraid she'd hit her head on something.

"What are you waiting for?" coaxed Ben.

"A little space. Move over, so I can fall on the rug."

Hector and Ben cleared a path for her. Then Katie held her breath, closed her eyes and keeled over. Ben heard her head make a loud klunk on the floor. Had she really passed out from the fall? But as Katie lay on the ground, she gave him a little wink.

Within moments, Omar came rushing forward to see what had happened.

"My heavens, what's wrong with the child?"

Katie lay limp, trying to look pale and weak. And trying hardest of all to keep her eyes closed.

"Low blood sugar," Ben explained. "She can konk out like this any time."

Omar was clearly concerned. "This is dreadful. Is there nothing to be done for the child? A glass of water, perhaps?"

"Yeah, do you have some?"

"Certainly. There's a sink in the other room."

So far, so good, thought Ben. The plan was working.

Omar hurried toward the door hidden behind the tapestry. Placing a key in the lock, he opened it. He quickly returned with a glass of water. Ben made sure to notice he'd left the door unlocked.

Now for the second stage of the plan.

"She also needs something sweet," said Ben. "A cookie, maybe? That'll perk her up in no time. I don't suppose you have any?"

"A sweet?" asked Omar. "Unfortunately not. I believe there is a grocery shop some blocks away. Perhaps I could purchase some there?"

"Right," said Hector. "You go get cookies. We'll take care of our darling Katie."

Once Omar had hurried from the shop, all three children congratulated themselves on the cleverness of their scheme.

Hector couldn't help laughing. "That guy'll be gone forever, finding cookies."

"Well we don't have forever," said Ben. "We've gotta get in that room right now."

Quickly, they approached the door Omar had left unlocked. Pushing it open, they peeked inside.

The sight that greeted their eyes filled them with horror.

In the center of the room was a long metal dissecting table. It was covered with sharp instruments and ominous-looking knives.

Resting on the table was the skeleton of a cat. Stretched across the wall was a white fur skin. It looked exactly like the soft white fur belonging to Melvin.

"Oh my gosh," gasped Hector. "That crazy guy must've chopped Melvin up in a million pieces!"

7

Katie and Ben hated to admit it, but it looked like Hector was right.

Poor Melvin had been murdered!

"But why?" asked Katie. "Why did Omar do it? He said he *loved* cats."

"That's why," Hector explained. "He's a cat *freak*! Maybe he's gonna take poor Melvin's bones and bury them in that temple at Boomerang he told us about. Poor Melvin's gonna be a *mummy*. It's just like in that movie, Katie. Some crazy Egyptian guy was chasing around this girl he loved so's he could turn her into a mummy, too. It's some crazy kind of mummy fever, I guess."

49

Ben had an awful thought. "You don't suppose Omar is a mummy himself, do you? He looks awfully wrinkly to me."

"You're right," Hector agreed. "These mummy guys can bring themselves back to life, ya know. All they've gotta do is say some dopey words and they pop right out of the grave, wearing their mummy rags."

"Don't talk crazy," said Katie. "It looks like Melvin is dead. What'll we do now?"

Ben thought a moment. "Maybe we should take his fur and bones back to Mr. Henderson, as evidence. At least the poor thing deserves a decent burial."

Hector glanced at the white fur skin stretched across the wall. *"I'm* not touching it! Suppose it's cursed."

Ben noticed the stack of boxes piled underneath the dissecting table. "Do you suppose old Melvin's eyes are in there?" he asked morbidly. "And all his insides, too? We better check."

Ben started dragging out one of the boxes.

Watching him, Katie felt her stomach roll over. She was afraid she might throw up.

"Let's get out of here," she pleaded. "I can't stand to see any more."

Suddenly a threatening voice shouted at them from the doorway.

"I warned you not to come in here!"

Omar had returned.

His vengeful eyes burned with anger.

Hector felt faint.

The mummy's vengeance would soon destroy them all!

For a moment, all three children were speechless. Ben stared at Omar's wrinkled face. Was he truly a mummy, come back to life?

Hector was certain of it.

Suddenly, the realization of the awful deed Omar had performed, made Katie angry. And bold.

"You terrible man," she shouted, "how could you do such a thing?"

Omar's fury was quickly controlled. "I realize such things are distasteful to some. That is why this room is locked. You children should not have disobeyed my wishes. You disappoint me."

"*Us?*" yelled Hector. "That's a laugh."

"I find nothing amusing. Clearly, this child was not ill at all. That was merely a clever scheme to get inside my private room, was it not? Why do you have such great interest in my hobby?"

51

Katie couldn't believe her ears. "You call this a hobby?"

"A business then. I admit I accept a fee for my services. But I only oblige very special clients."

"So that's it," said Katie. "Well, who paid you to kill poor Melvin?"

Omar seemed both surprised and offended. *"Kill?* What is this talk of killing?"

"C'mon," said Hector, "come clean. We caught you red handed. This place is a torture chamber, and you're a cat killer!"

The children stared as the Egyptian suddenly began to laugh. Katie feared Omar might be going crazy. Hector was doubly convinced he was some insane mummy, come back to life.

"Now I understand your apprehension," Omar replied. "These instruments you see displayed are the tools of my trade . . . taxidermy. I do not torture living things. I preserve those cherished animals who have passed on. Often, their owners cannot bear to be parted from them."

By way of explanation, Omar opened several of the boxes that rested underneath the table. In each was a lifelike-looking cat, carefully and lovingly preserved.

"This old gentleman," he explained, gesturing to a large marmalade cat, "was known as Napoleon. He served his master well for sixteen years. Now, after death, he shall have an honored place in his old home forever."

"You mean you stuff dead things?" asked Ben.

"Stuffing is hardly an accurate term," Omar corrected. "Taxidermy is an ancient art, now usually only practiced by highly skilled museum personnel. Years ago, I worked for such a museum in Cairo. But now, I have this gallery. Here, my customers are mainly interested in fine objects of art. They might consider my craft distasteful, so I do not advertise. Only select clients are aware of my auxiliary business."

Hector didn't get the drift of everything Omar said. "Does that mean you didn't cut up Melvin?"

"Goodness, no. It should be obvious, I have great reverence for cats."

"Then why'd you sneak out of the cat show?" asked Ben.

"Like yourself, I wished to meet the world's most talented, unique feline. But a business appointment caused me to leave in haste. I understand Melvin has since been taken from his owner. My dearest hope is that he be returned, unharmed. No one from my country would inflict harm upon a feline. We are a people of ancient traditions. In times of old, *all* cats, not only sacred ones, were revered and protected. The killing of a cat was punishable by *death*. This is because it was considered a far more grievous crime to kill a cat than to kill a human. So you see, such a deed would be unthinkable."

Ben still wasn't convinced. "I don't know. If you didn't stuff Melvin, why'd you say you wanted to add him to your collection?"

Omar smiled. "My collection of *pets*, of course." Proudly, he produced a large collection of photographs from his pocket. They were all of cats.

"I have seventeen at home," he explained. "I was merely hoping I'd have an opportunity to take Melvin's photograph. Of course, my pets are only of value to myself. Originally, they were all—how do you say it—strays. Yes, my seventeen little ones were all rescued from the street. But to me, they are as priceless as any of the art objects in my gallery. One cannot put an estimate on love and devotion, do you not agree?"

That's all Katie had to hear. She was instantly sorry for all the awful suspicions they'd had regarding Omar. He was actually one of them . . . a rescuer in search of kitties. Seventeen strays! That wasn't as many as R.I.S.K. had rescued, but it was a lot!

Katie glared at Hector. This was all his fault. His crazy talk about mummies had gotten them all carried away.

She jabbed him in the side. "You and your nutty ideas."

"Okay," he argued. "It was a false lead. So what?"

Omar looked confused. "I feel you children have not been candid about the nature of your visit. You have no true interest in my art objects after all, do you?"

"Heck no," admitted Hector. "We're on the trail of the catnapper."

Omar nodded. "Ah, now I see. In that case, let me wish you luck in your quest. I, too, wish for Melvin's safe return." Reaching into one of the glass cases, he removed a small charm on a satin cord. "Perhaps you will accept this? It may be of aid to you."

Dangling from the cord was a small gold pendant in the shape of a cat. Omar handed it to Katie.

"Gosh, thanks. It's very pretty. Is it gold?"

"The metal is not precious," Omar explained. "But the good luck that accompanies it is most valuable."

Katie placed the pendant around her neck. Before leaving the shop, the children thanked the Egyptian man for being so understanding. Even Hector agreed that Omar had turned out to be a "good egg."

"But we need more than luck," he added as they walked down the street. "We need fast action. Omar is scratched off our list of suspects. That only leaves Barney Carter, and the reporter on TV said he won't talk to anyone. How're we gonna get to see him?"

"No problem," said Ben. "He owns a barber shop, right?"

"Yeah," said Katie, giving Hector a piercing glance. Then she pulled the baseball cap from his head. "I've just decided something, brother dear. You're badly in need of a haircut!"

8

Katie and Ben hurried along the streets until they found a drug store. There, they stopped to check through the phone book. They found the address for Carter's Clip Joint.

Hector trailed along behind. He hated haircuts. And he didn't need one. He had just gotten his hair nicely thick and long, so his baseball cap didn't slide over his ears. They were big ears, too, which always stuck out after a haircut.

"*You* get your hair cut, Ben," he grumbled.

"I had mine done last week. Besides, Katie and I already voted. Two against one. You're the candidate for the barber chair."

Hector groaned. Democratic voting stunk!

At the next executive meeting of R.I.S.K., he was going to vote to abolish it!

Carter's Clip Joint was over on the east side, the other end of town. That meant more bus fares. Between them, Katie and Ben had only two dollars and thirteen cents, not enough for carfare and a haircut.

"How much cash do you have?" she asked Hector.

"Just a little," he said evasively.

"How little?"

"A dime."

Katie knew that was a lie. Hector *always* had money stashed in his sneaker. "Come clean," she ordered.

"I won't!"

Katie knew what to do. She began tickling Hector under his arms unmercifully, until he started kicking frantically. That's when Ben pulled off his sneaker and found several dollar bills hidden neatly inside.

"Look at all this loot," he shouted. "It's a fortune."

"It's only eight dollars. Miss Barclay paid me in advance."

"Well, it's enough for a haircut." Katie shoved the money in her pocket.

Hector was furious. "You can't steal my money to cut my hair," he whined.

"Sure we can. And don't tell Mom and Dad. Or I'll tell them you tried to blackmail us."

"That's bribery!"

Ben smiled. "Yeah, we know. We learned it from you."

Hector continued to protest, but Katie ignored him. "It's all for a good cause. You're the one who wanted to help find Melvin."

Good cause, baloney! It was a stinking deal. So far, Hector's free advertising had cost him eight dollars.

He was still looking sullen when they arrived outside Carter's Clip Joint. Though it was early afternoon, there was a sign in the barber shop window saying CLOSED.

Katie peeked through the window and noticed Barney Carter seated in back of the shop.

"Guess he locked himself in to get away from all the reporters."

Ben began banging on the door. At first, Carter ignored the pounding. But when it didn't stop, he was forced to come to the entrance.

"Can't you read?" he shouted, throwing open the door.

"Sure," said Ben, "but this is an emergency. This kid needs a haircut immediately."

Carter frowned. "An emergency haircut?"

"That's right," said Katie, thinking quickly. "We're leaving the country today. Our folks are taking us to Russia. But Dad says he doesn't want Communists cutting his son's hair."

"Sorry, I'm closed. There's another shop a few blocks down."

"But we heard you're the best," said Ben. He pulled the baseball cap from Hector's head. "And you see what bad shape this kid is in."

Barney Carter stared at Hector's hair with professional concern. "You're right, he looks awful. Okay, I'll do a quick job on him, but I've gotta make it fast. I'm expecting an important phone call any minute. When it comes, I've gotta go."

As Carter opened the door, Katie and Ben hurried into the shop, dragging Hector along behind. He hadn't liked that crack about his hair. Only a crooked catnapper would make such a lousy remark! Reluctantly, he settled in the barber chair as Carter wrapped a towel around his neck.

Katie glanced around the place, hoping to find some evidence that a cat was hidden somewhere. There was so much hair scattered on the floor, it was impossible to tell if any of it belonged to a cat. She noticed a small back room off the main shop. Could Melvin be hidden inside?

For a professional barber, Barney Carter seemed awfully ill at ease. Hector noticed his hands shaking as he proceeded to clip great chunks of hair from the sides of his head. He'd seen poodles get better cuts!

Katie noticed the man's obvious nervousness, as well. What was he afraid of?

She tried appearing casual. "Say, you look familiar. Have we met before? I know; I saw you at the pet show yesterday."

Carter stared at her suspiciously. "What of it?"

"Oh nothing. It's just that I never forget a face. I guess you heard about what happened to that poor cat, Melvin. Wasn't that terrible?"

At the mere mention of Melvin's name, Carter grew angry. He started chopping away at Hector's hair with a vengeance.

"Justice is what I call it," he said sternly. "Victor Henderson stole that cat in the first place. Now someone stole it from him. I wouldn't lose any sleep over it."

Maybe not, but Hector thought he was losing far too much hair. Glancing at himself in the mirror, he thought it looked as if he were being scalped!

Ben sat in the barber chair beside him, hoping to keep Carter talking. "I think I've seen your picture in the paper. Sure, aren't you the guy who sold Melvin to Mr. Henderson?"

"I *never* sold Melvin," Carter shouted. "That's a filthy lie Henderson has been spreading around town. But he'll pay for it, you'll see."

Wow, thought Katie; Carter was starting to incriminate himself. Too bad they hadn't brought a tape recorder.

"I don't understand," she continued, "It said in the newspaper—"

"Don't believe everything you read in the papers, girlie. Those reporters don't wanna hear the truth. That's why I won't let them in my shop. They've been pestering me all day. No, they're only interested in headlines, not facts."

"Well, what are the facts?" asked Ben.

"They're none of your business, that's what. But if you must know, I got a dirty deal. Vic Henderson is king of the dirty deals. Back when I knew him, he was a gambler and a two-bit salesman, always trying to swindle someone.

Vic sold anything: bum cars, phony real estate. And boy, did he sell me a bill of goods."

"What do you mean?" asked Ben.

"Well, I'd found this cat at my back door a few weeks earlier. He was skinny and starving. But I took a liking to him. I gave him a home and named him Melvin. I guess I liked him because he had a real strange way of talking. I'd never heard a cat meow like that before. Anyway, Henderson was over one day. He noticed how different Melvin's meow was, too. That's when he told me there was an ad agency looking for a special cat for their commercials. He said he knew some guy up there who could put in a good word for Melvin. He told me he'd take my cat over and bring him back in a day or two. But that's the last I saw of him *or* Melvin. I figured the cat had run away from him or something. Heck, he was only a stray, so I didn't bother much about it. A year later, I see Melvin on the television. Then I hear he's worth a million bucks. Boy, was I boiling!"

By this time, Hector was boiling, too. Barney Carter had gotten so excited telling his story, he'd cut both sides of Hector's hair inches shorter than the back.

"Hey mister, what're you trying to do, give me a pony tail?"

"Look, I said I was in a hurry. Why are you kids asking so many questions, anyhow? Did those reporters send you snooping around here? If they did . . ."

Before the children could deny everything, the phone in the back room started to ring. Carter quickly threw down his scissors and went hurrying to answer it.

"He's definitely our man," whispered Katie. "You heard him say Melvin was worth a million. That's exactly how much he asked for in that ransom note."

Ben agreed. "But we have no proof. First, we'll have to find out where he's hidden Melvin."

Hector stared at his lopsided head of hair. "First get him back to finish this! I look like an Indian!"

Ben glanced at the back room. "I wonder who he's talking to on the phone. An accomplice, maybe?"

"Let's listen," said Katie.

Cautiously they tiptoed toward the door, where Carter was in a heated conversation.

"No, that's not good enough," he shouted

into the phone. "I won't wait any longer. Before I'm finished, Henderson won't have a dime. *I* make the decisions. You follow my orders, or I get someone else."

Yes, Carter was definitely talking with his accomplice.

"You suppose they're arranging the ransom pick-up?" asked Ben.

Katie nodded. "Guess he's too smart to be caught with the money himself."

"Okay," Carter continued, "we're all set. No, don't come here. I think those lousy reporters are still snooping around my place. I'll meet you in half and hour on the corner of Mercer Street. Then we'll make the final arrangements."

Hurriedly, the children ran from the door as Carter hung up the phone.

"Sorry," he said, throwing on his jacket. "I don't have time to finish that cut. I've gotta run."

"What d'ya mean?" Hector grumbled. "I can't go through life like this."

Katie shoved Hector's cap on his head. "That's okay. We've gotta get to Russia anyhow. What do we owe you?"

Hector poked his sister. "Don't you give that

guy a dime. He's a butcher, not a barber. And I don't believe a word he said. The only honest thing he ever did is name this place the Clip Joint."

Carter was growing impatient. "Listen, I'm closing up now. You kids better scram. The haircut's on the house; just get moving."

As Barney Carter hurried for the door, Hector took one final look at his mutilated hair. He'd be laughed right off the baseball field!

Carter quickly locked the shop, then hailed a cab.

"We've gotta follow him," said Katie.

They hopped into the next taxi that came along. "Follow that cab," she shouted to the driver.

"Say, what's the big joke, kid?"

"Never mind," said Ben. "Just take us to the corner of Mercer Street, okay?"

Fifteen minutes and five dollars later, the taxi pulled up on Mercer Street. The children dashed out and took cover underneath the awning of a book shop. There, they pretended to browse through the sidewalk stalls of books. Secretly, they observed Barney Carter. He was standing on the corner, pacing back and forth, obviously waiting for someone.

After several minutes, a man wearing dark glasses and smoking a cigar stepped from his car. Assured no one was watching, he approached Carter.

Hector was certain he was a definite gangster type. "That's why they all wear dark glasses. They have to hide their sneaky, beady eyes."

Carter and the stranger engaged in noisy conversation. But not quite noisy enough for the children to hear. So accidentally on purpose, Katie dropped a book on the sidewalk. Bending over to retrieve it, she inched closer to Carter and his companion. Now she could hear every word they said.

"Look, Barney, this isn't going to be easy," the man warned. "Maybe if you come down in price."

"A million bucks and not a penny less," Carter argued. "I'll get even with Henderson if it's the last thing I do."

"But I've never handled a deal this big before."

"What's the matter, scared? Afraid of a little risk? Say, if you don't want your ten percent . . ."

"No, I'll go through with it. But it's a chancy business."

67

"Guys in your business are supposed to take chances. You get the rest of those papers ready . . . fast."

Katie hurried back to Ben and Hector. "They're making arrangements for the ransom instructions," she explained. "I'll bet Mr. Henderson gets another note real soon. I'm sure it'll tell where to leave the money."

"It's time we called in the police," said Ben. "We can't handle something this big by ourselves."

Katie agreed. They watched Dark Glasses get into his car. Before he drove off, Katie quickly jotted down his license number. Then Barney Carter hailed another cab, which disappeared down the crowded street.

The children hurried to the corner phone booth. They called the local precinct and asked to speak with Detective McCullough. Katie explained all about their unofficial investigation and the super evidence they'd come across.

"Carter is the catnapper," she said excitedly. "And the man in dark glasses is his accomplice. He's gonna deliver the second ransom note. If you hurry, you can catch him red-handed!"

There was a long silence on the other end of the phone.

"That's all very interesting," said the detective finally. "I don't know that I believe it, but it sure sounds interesting."

"But it's true!"

"Maybe so, little girl, but my hands are tied. At the request of Mr. Henderson, I've been ordered off the case. I'm not allowed to investigate further."

Katie was furious. "Don't you guys want to catch the catnapper?"

"Sorry, but I have to obey orders. I'll check out that license plate for you, though *unofficially*, of course. Meanwhile, I suggest you kids go home. There's nothing you can do on your own but get into big trouble."

Disgustedly, Katie slammed down the phone.

"What'd he say?" asked Hector, eagerly. "Are the cops gonna zero in on those thieves? Did you tell 'em to bring handcuffs? And tear gas? Oh wow, I can't wait for the big showdown!"

"Forget it," she shouted. "The police don't care a thing about poor Melvin. They refuse to listen. We'll have to catch those guys ourselves!"

9

Was everything lost?

Who was Dark Glasses?

Where had he gone?

They'd wasted precious time, trying to get the police involved.

"Maybe we should call Herbie Rappaport," suggested Hector. "He's a real pal since I let him join R.I.S.K. We also swap crime comics, so he's an expert, too. After all, we're gonna need someone's help."

Katie shrugged. "Some help. We can do without whiny little Herbie, thank you. No, we have only one choice left. We've gotta get to

71

Victor Henderson and tell him everything we know. If we don't hurry, he'll be out a million dollars!"

With the money remaining, the children took a bus, which let them off outside the Camelot Hotel. Rushing through the lobby, they asked for Henderson's room number, then took the elevator to the third floor.

Hector pressed the elevator button. "I can't believe the cops could be so stupid. They're always real sharp in stories."

"I guess it's not their fault," said Ben philosophically. "After all, Henderson ordered them off the case. And I don't blame him. Carter's got a terrible temper. Maybe Henderson suspected he was the catnapper and was afraid he'd do something awful to Melvin. Chop him up or something."

"Yeah," Hector agreed, "just like he did to my hair."

Katie knocked on the door of room 312, and Victor Henderson answered. There were dark circles under his eyes, and he looked very nervous. In fact, he looked as if he hadn't slept all night.

"Yeah, what is it?"

"We met you at the cat show yesterday, remember?" asked Ben.

"Oh, yeah."

"Can we come in? We've got important news about Melvin."

Henderson seemed frightened. "Melvin? What could you know about Melvin?"

"We know who stole him," said Hector.

A tall, distinguished-looking gray-haired man came to the door. "What is it, Victor?"

Katie recognized him immediately from television. He was Hartley Reese, the president of Meow Chow.

"These kids say they have information about Melvin."

"Well, let them in."

Hector was bursting to talk. "Barney Carter snatched your cat. We heard him talking to his accomplice. He admitted he wanted a million bucks."

Neither Henderson or Reese seemed surprised.

"I suspected as much," said Hartley Reese.

"You mean you know it's Carter?" asked Katie in surprise.

"We've got no proof," Henderson explained. "Carter's too shifty for that. But I figured Melvin was taken by someone he knew. Otherwise, my cat might've put up a fuss. He can yell really loud when he wants to. Anyway, I told Mr. Reese all about my trouble with Carter. That guy won't admit he sold me Melvin, fair and square. We both figured he's the only one mean enough to snatch my cat."

"I don't get it," said Hector. "If you *know* Carter did it, why'd you call off the cops?"

Hartley Reese explained. "Knowing it and proving it are two different things. Right now, all we're interested in is Melvin's safe return. If Mr. Carter knows we suspect him, he might kill the cat, just to get even. No, Melvin is too valuable to my company to take such risks. Once he's been returned, safe and sound, then we'll call in the authorities and tell them what we know."

"But he won't be returned," said Katie. "Not unless you pay a million dollars."

"We fully intend to do so," said Mr. Reese. "Melvin is worth ten times that to my company. We're about to market a new Melvin video game and several new toys for distribution this Christmas. With the international sales included, we could gross over ten million in profit. Ten percent of that is a small price to pay."

"So we're gonna pay it," said Henderson.

"Well, my company will," corrected Mr.

Reese. "I was on the telephone most of the night arranging the transaction. Then we had to wait for the money to arrive. The latest note specified the denominations. One million dollars in fifty-dollar bills."

"Unmarked," Henderson added. "Carter's note insisted on that."

"So you got another note?" asked Katie.

Victor Henderson explained it had been slipped under his hotel door earlier. Katie was now positive the man in dark glasses had placed it there.

"Did you recognize the handwriting?" asked Ben.

"No, this one is typed."

Henderson took the note from his pocket to show the children:

HERE ARE YOUR INSTRUCTIONS. I WANT THE CASH IN FIFTY-DOLLAR BILLS. ALL UNMARKED. LEAVE THE MILLION BUCKS IN A LARGE BROWN PAPER BAG BY ULYSSES GRANT'S MONUMENT IN RIVERSIDE PARK. COME ALONE. BE THERE AT SIX O'CLOCK. IF ALL GOES ACCORDING TO PLAN, YOU'LL FIND MELVIN ON YOUR DOOR-

STEP IN THE MORNING. ANY SLIP-UPS, AND MELVIN WILL BE CHOPPED TO PIECES AND SHOVED IN A BOX OF MEOW CHOW.

"How terrible," said Katie.

Hector fiddled with his hair. "How typical. That guy loves chopping things up."

"Gee, there must be something we can do," said Ben. "We can't let Carter get away with this."

"The decision has already been made," said Mr. Reese emphatically. "I want no police following Mr. Henderson. The money will be paid, every cent. It's all ready and waiting in that suitcase."

Hector gulped. "A million dollars? In that suitcase? Can I look?"

Slowly, almost reverently, Hector approached the bed. He stared down at the mountains of cash resting inside the suitcase. Thousands of crisp new green bills. How he'd love to wiggle his fingers through it. His toes, too. Hundreds of engravings of President Grant stared back at him. He couldn't help wishing at least a few were his.

"At least that lousy Carter has a sense of

humor," he noted. "He asked you to leave the cash by Grant's Monument, right? Well, Grant's picture is on all these bills. Funny, eh?"

"I fail to see any humor in this," chided Hartley Reese. "As soon as Melvin is safely returned, Mr. Carter will get what he deserves. In the meantime, I request that you children hold this information in the strictest confidence. We can't have our fox going to ground, can we?"

"You can trust us," Katie assured him. "We're just as worried about Melvin as you are."

Victor Henderson checked his watch, then began pacing the room. "I hope I can last until six o'clock. This business is making me a nervous wreck. I didn't sleep at all last night. I kept thinking I heard poor Melvin meowing in my ear, crying for me to help him."

Just then, Katie heard the faint sound of a meow in the distance, herself. "Gosh, I must be cracking up. I can hear Melvin, too."

Mr. Reese smiled. "No, my dear, you're not imagining things."

Hartley Reese pointed toward four wicker baskets, resting in the corner of the room. Inside each one was a large cat: two tabbies, one marmalade and one black.

"These are Melvin's traveling companions," he explained. "Whenever Melvin does a guest appearance, like the one at the cat show yesterday, my company pays his air fare into town."

"That's right," added Mr. Henderson. "But Melvin hates traveling alone; it makes him nervous. So I always bring my other cats to keep him company."

Ben giggled. "What do you know. I've heard of rock groupies, but never *cat* groupies."

"I call them Melvin's cousins," said Henderson. "Melvin gets real antsy if his friends aren't around. The only problem is, they hate traveling. Planes make them sick. My vet usually prescribes a sedative to calm them down."

As Katie strolled over to the cats to take a closer look, Henderson continued pacing the room.

"Take it easy, Victor," advised Mr. Reese. "It looks as if *you're* the one who needs a sedative. Don't worry; everything will go according to plan."

"I can't help worrying. When I think of that guy Carter holding Melvin for ransom, it makes my blood boil. When this is over, I'm gonna put him behind bars."

"And we'll help you do it," said Katie, stroking the marmalade cat. It rolled over sleepily, without opening its eyes. "Don't worry," she soothed, "your cousin will be home soon."

Katie also petted the tabbies and the black cat. The black cat seemed the most sluggish of all. After stroking his tummy a while, he slowly opened his eyes. He seemed attracted to Katie, staring at her with bright blue eyes. Katie realized it was the pendant around her neck that drew his attention. She took it off and began by dangle it in front of him. He seemed almost hypnotized by the sparkling gold charm. Sleepily, he reached out a paw to grab it, and Katie continued tickling his tummy.

"Better not bother that one," Henderson cautioned. "That's Boris, and he's got stomach troubles. In fact, I think it's time he had another pill."

At the mention of the word "pill," Hector turned pale.

"Oh my gosh, I forgot all about Sebastian! He should've had his green pill hours ago. Miss Barclay said if he doesn't get them on time, he starts itching all over. I hope the dumb guy hasn't scratched himself to death!"

"I guess we better get home," said Katie. She gave the black cat some final tickles.

Hartley Reese showed them to the door. "I want to thank you children for your concern. And remember, I'm counting on your discretion. We mustn't have our delicate transaction disrupted. After Victor has rescued Melvin, we'll make sure justice is done."

"Don't worry," Ben assured him. "You can count on us."

As they left the room, Victor Henderson was still pacing apprehensively.

Hector was apprehensive, too. He couldn't wait to get home.

"I sure hope Sebastian hasn't dropped dead on me or something. Wow, what lousy advertising that would be!"

10

Nervously, Hector turned the key in Miss Barclay's door.

"You guys come in with me, okay? Just in case Sebastian is lying in a pool of blood or something."

"Don't talk stupid," said Katie. "I told you, that cat's a hypochondriac. Pink pills, green pills. I bet he doesn't need any of them."

The Siamese was seated on the Persian rug in the hallway. The moment he saw Hector, he let out a squeal, leaped in the air, then pounced on him.

Ben laughed. "He sure looks healthy to me."

Hurriedly, Hector chopped up two pills, burying them in some cat food. They watched as Sebastian gobbled it down.

"See," Ben reassured him, "you were worried about nothing."

Katie was worried, too. But not about Sebastian. Glancing into the cat's bright blue eyes, she could tell he was perfectly healthy. No, something else was bothering her. The whole catnapping caper didn't fit together right. There was a nagging doubt in the back of her mind. But she couldn't put her finger on it.

Returning home, she expressed her concern to Ben.

"You're just worried Barney Carter might get away. He's a sneaky devil, that's for sure. I only hope the cops can nab him with the loot. If he's got a chance to hide the million somewhere, he might just get away with it."

"I guess that's it," she agreed. "I know we promised not to interfere, but I still wish there was something we could do. How do we make sure Carter doesn't run off with the ransom?"

Hector agreed. "Yeah, what if he leaves the country? Then the cops'll never nab him. Maybe he'll open a barber shop in Europe or something. Pretty soon, everyone over there will be *bald!*"

Katie had a thought. "I'll bet Carter sends Dark Glasses to pick up the money. He's too smart to take that risk himself."

Ben didn't get it. "So?"

"So that means we can still do a little snooping on our own. Dark Glasses doesn't know who we are. What if we get to the park before the ransom pick-up time? Maybe we can spot him there? At least that would place him at the scene of the crime. Then when we give evidence, we can *prove* he's Carter's accomplice. The phone company will have a record of his call to Carter's shop."

"That's no good," said Ben. "It would be our word against his. Sure, maybe we can prove that Carter and Dark Glasses know each other. But we'd have to prove Dark Glasses came to pick up the ransom. He wouldn't confess on his own."

"A *picture* would be proof," shouted Katie. "We could take his *photograph*. Dark Glasses would never suspect us, and we'd have real evidence in full color."

Ben seemed uneasy. "That sounds dangerous."

Hector was all for it. He loved the idea of

danger. But getting back at Barney Carter for his stinking haircut was even more important.

"Carter's gotta go to jail," he insisted. "That bum belongs behind bars!"

So, it was agreed. The children would get to the park at five o'clock and begin "staking out" the area.

Katie ran to the closet for her camera, making sure it was loaded with film.

Then they checked the kitchen clock.

"We'd better move," said Ben. "It's almost five now."

As they hurried toward the door, Mrs. Morrison returned from shopping.

"Where have you kids been all day? And where are you going now?"

"To the park, Mom," explained Katie. "To take some pictures."

"Pictures? Of what?"

"Of Hector's new haircut, of course."

Mrs. Morrison stared at her son. "What on earth! Don't tell me Sam, our barber, did *that*!"

"No," said Katie, dragging Hector from the room. "We went to a new place. Don't you love it? It's the latest style; all the kids are getting it done. It's called the Iroquois."

86

11

_____

"I don't really look like an Indian, do I?" grumbled Hector.

"Shut up," Ben ordered, "and keep your head down."

The children sat hidden behind a row of bushes, several yards away from Grant's Monument. Opposite the statue were rows of benches. An old woman was seated on one, feeding the pigeons. In the center of the granite walk, a young man with an easel was painting a picture of the statue.

Dark Glasses was nowhere in sight.

"Suppose you have this figured wrong?" Ben

whispered. "The ransom note said six o'clock. Maybe no one's gonna show up this early."

"He has to," Katie reasoned. "Dark Glasses will check the place out, to make sure no police are around."

Hector thought the pigeon lady looked suspicious.

"She could be a guy in a skirt. You know, we never really saw Dark Glasses' eyes. And my art teacher says that eyes are the most important part of a face. Eyes identify your personality."

Katie and Ben sneered.

"Well okay, but maybe she's Barney Carter's mother. I bet she's just as rotten as he is."

After several minutes of waiting, Katie grew uneasy. Was it possible she had things figured wrong? Perhaps Barney Carter would pick up the ransom himself? In that case, it was vital that they stay hidden.

Katie checked her camera again, making sure the flash was set and ready. Peering through the bushes, the children watched the artist continue his painting. As he put on the finishing touches, an old man passed by. His clothes were ragged and dirty, and he looked like a bum. A drunken bum, most likely. He knocked into the easel and spilled some of the young man's paint. A bottle of gray splattered along the ground. But the bum took no notice. He began rummaging through a garbage can nearby.

Was he Dark Glasses in disguise?

Perhaps.

"Sure," said Ben. "It's a perfect cover. No one would suspect a bum, rummaging around. When Henderson drops the paper bag, I bet that guy picks it up."

"No, he's leaving," said Katie. She watched him disappear behind some trees. "False alarm."

The pigeon lady got up to leave, too.

Then the young man closed up his easel and strolled down the path, toward the exit.

Dusk was beginning to fall, and it seemed the park was now deserted. A chilly wind blew through the bushes. The three of them were growing nervous, yet none of them would admit that to the others. They sat huddled in silence . . . waiting.

Suddenly, a large hand seemed to appear from nowhere. It clamped itself on Katie's shoulder.

It was the old bum.

Katie quickly pulled away. "What do you want?" she asked, trembling.

"Got a dime?"

She stared into the bum's wrinkled old face. Could it be Dark Glasses?

"Go away," said Ben. "We have no money."

"That's what they all say," he grumbled. Then he staggered along down the path.

"Wow, what a close call," sighed Ben. "For a minute, I thought he was—"

"Me, too," gasped Katie. "I guess all this talk about disguises has made me too suspicious."

Changing position, Katie glanced down at her shoulder. Somehow, the bum had smeared gray paint all over it.

"Darn, look at my shirt; it's ruined. That old guy must have gotten paint all over himself when he bumped into the easel."

"Yeah, you're a mess," said Hector. "Look, it's all over your hand, too."

Katie glanced at the palm of her right hand. It was smeared with a black, inky substance. "That's strange. I didn't notice any black in that picture. Anyway, this looks like different kind of paint. I wonder how...."

A sudden realization flashed through Katie's mind. "Hector, what'd you say earlier about eyes?"

"Huh? You mean what my art teacher said? She told us eyes are the most important part of a face."

"And she was right!" shouted Katie, excitedly. "Now I know what's been bothering me. Listen, Ben, we've gotta get out of here . . . fast. We've gotta get back to the hotel before Mr. Henderson delivers that money!"

12

A taxi!

That's what Katie needed . . . and fast.

She checked her pockets. Empty.

Quickly running across the street from River-side Park, she hailed one down, anyway. There was no time to worry about a few dollars when a million was at stake. Without explaining, she practically shoved Hector and Ben into the backseat.

"Take us to the Camelot Hotel," she shouted. "And hurry. This is an emergency!"

Hector stared at his sister. He'd never seen her so excited before. What was up?

"What a dope I've been," she mumbled. "What a jerk."

He gave her a sickening grin. "Is that what you just discovered? Gosh, Katie, I could've told you that. I've always known—"

"Oh, shut up. We've *all* been jerks. We had the evidence right in front of our eyes, but we didn't know it."

Ben was growing impatient. "If I've been a jerk, I'd like to know *why*. When are you gonna tell us what you're *talking* about? Why'd you make us leave the park? I thought we were going to catch the thief red-handed."

"We are, Ben. But he's not gonna be in the park. That's why we've gotta get back to Henderson's hotel in time. If we don't—"

"Three bucks, kids," said the driver, pulling up in front of the Camelot Hotel.

"We'll pay you next time," said Katie, hurriedly opening the door.

She dashed out as fast as she could, with Hector and Ben in close pursuit.

"Come back here, you kids," he shouted. "Pay up or you're in trouble."

"I told you we should've called Herbie Rappaport," Hector panted. "His dad is a *cab driver*."

The driver rushed from his cab and started

chasing the children into the hotel lobby. "Give me my dough or I call the cops!"

"Terrific," yelled Katie as she pushed her way past several people. "Call Detective McCullough at the Twentieth Precinct. Get him to come over here immediately. Tell him it's about Melvin."

The taxi driver stood in stunned confusion as the hotel's elevator doors closed quickly behind the children.

Ben refused to wait another moment for an explanation. "Swell, now *we're* thieves, too. Katie, spill what you know and fast."

"Not yet, Ben. Gosh, I wish I knew the time. I hope Henderson hasn't left with the ransom money yet."

The elevator seemed maddeningly slow. First, it stopped on the second floor, where three people got out. Katie thought she'd burst before it finally let them off on the third floor.

Rushing down the hall, she almost tripped over the carpeting. As she was about to knock on the door of room 312, Victor Henderson emerged. He was carrying a large brown paper bag tucked under his arm.

"Thank goodness we got here in time," she gasped.

"What are you kids doing back here?" he asked. "I'm just on my way to the park to drop off the money as arranged."

"No, you can't go yet," Katie protested.

Hartley Reese, who was still inside the hotel room, came to the door.

"What are you children doing back here? I thought I explained the delicacy of this transaction."

"We know all about that," said Ben. "But Katie insists she knows something important."

"Whatever it is will have to wait," insisted Mr. Reese. "If we ever hope to get Melvin back—"

"Look, I'm leaving," shouted Henderson, checking his watch. "It's almost six o'clock."

"No you're not," said Katie. "Not until you hear me out."

As the two men continued protesting, Katie raised the camera she had strapped around her neck. She began taking several snapshots in quick succession. The blinding light of the flashbulbs took Henderson and Reese by surprise. As they raised their hands to their eyes, Katie started pushing them both back into the hotel room. All the while, she continued snapping more and more pictures.

Still not knowing why, Hector and Ben started pushing the men, too.

"Look, Ben, there's a key inside the door," she yelled. "Grab it fast and hide it somewhere."

"Okay, but I hope you know what you're doing."

Ben quickly turned the key in the lock. Then he ran toward the window and threw it out.

"You crazy kids," screamed Henderson. "You've ruined everything."

"This is disgraceful," protested Mr. Reese. "Do you realize what you've done? If Victor doesn't get to the park on time with the money, Melvin may be *murdered*!"

Henderson agreed. "Yeah, you read Carter's note. My cat'll wind up in Meow Chow."

Hartley Reese rushed toward the telephone. "I'm calling hotel security. We've got to get that door unlocked. If we hurry, perhaps there's still time to save Melvin."

"Don't bother," said Katie. "Because I know exactly where Melvin is this very minute."

Henderson and Reese stared at Katie.

So did Ben and Hector.

"I think Katie's flipped out," mumbled Hector.

"No I haven't. In fact, *you* gave me my biggest clue, Hector."

"I did?"

"Sure. You said *eyes* were the key to a person's identity. Well, you were right, and it goes for cats, too. When you were feeding Sebastian, I noticed his bright blue eyes. It seemed as if they were telling me something, and finally I remembered something important. Only Siamese cats have eyes like that. And sometimes, white shorthairs. But never black cats. Black cats always have orange or yellow eyes. It's Mother Nature's rule."

"What's she babbling about?" shouted Henderson. "The kid is crazy!"

Ben had to agree. It *did* sound like babbling. "What do you mean, Katie? You *can't* know where Melvin is. We've been together all day, and we never saw him."

"Yes you did."

"Well where is he?" asked. Hector, eagerly. "Back at Carter's Clip Joint?"

"No, he's right here. He's been in this room all the time. In fact, he was never missing. That's him over there, sleeping in the basket."

Frowning, Hartley Reese shook his head. "This child is demented." He began dialing the phone. "I'm calling security. And the hotel's doctor. Perhaps there's a psychiatrist on staff, as well."

"Oh, I'm not crazy," she insisted. "I can prove it."

Hurrying into the bathroom, Katie returned with a wet washcloth. Approaching the basket where the large black cat lay sleeping, she began to stroke him with the wet cloth.

Within moments, a large section of the cat's fur had transformed itself. It was no longer black but white! The cat meeowed softly, then rolled over.

Triumphantly, Katie held up the cloth for inspection. It was totally covered in black. "I guess it's some kind of vegetable dye," she explained. "It must've come off on my hand when I petted the cat earlier. But I didn't notice it at first. Then that old bum bumped into me in the park and smeared gray paint all over my shirt. But this stuff on my hands seemed different. That's when I remembered the artist in the park wasn't using black in his picture. So it must've come from someplace else."

Hector glared at Hartley Reese. At last, the crime was solved. "Say, now I get it," he said, smugly. "Pretty sneaky, Mr. Meow Chow. I bet you thought you'd get a fortune's worth of free publicity by pretending Melvin had been stolen. Shame on you . . . a president and everything."

"Hey, none of this makes sense," said Henderson. "Why would anyone switch cats on me? And what happened to Boris?"

"There is no Boris," said Katie.

"I won't listen to another word," argued Hartley Reese. "That can't be Melvin. If it were, I'd recognize him."

"Would you? Most cats look alike when they're asleep. Take a closer look."

Hartley Reese bent over the basket where the cat lay sleeping. The cat's sedative was slowly wearing off. He rolled over, stretched out one paw and let out a faint meow. Faint as it was, the sound was unmistakable. It sounded almost as if the cat were saying, "Meow Chow."

"It *is* Melvin!" gasped Mr. Reese, lifting the cat into his arms. "I can't believe it. And I can't possibly understand it."

"Say, who are you fooling?" shouted Hector.

"No, you've got it figured wrong," Katie explained. "Mr. Reese isn't our man. Victor Henderson, here, stole his own cat."

Now Hector was truly confused. *"Henderson? I thought it was the other guy."*

"Hey, now I get it," said Ben. "Henderson dipped Melvin in some kind of dye and drugged him so he wouldn't make any noise. Then he pretended he was another cat altogether. It would've been real easy for him to slip out of the cat show with Melvin. He rushed the cat over here to his hotel. Then he returned to the show and said Melvin had been stolen. No one would suspect a person of stealing his own cat."

"That's right," said Katie. "And that's what you were counting on, wasn't it, Mr. Henderson? You wrote those ransom notes yourself, didn't you? You never intended to take that money to the park at all. That's why you wanted to make sure the police didn't follow you. You planned to hide the cash somewhere. Then in the morning, after Melvin's sedative wore off and he was all cleaned up, you could tell Mr. Reese you found Melvin on your doorstep."

"Pretty clever," said Ben. "By tomorrow, you'd be one million dollars richer."

Hector was still confused. "If all this is true, what's Barney Carter have to do with it? And who the heck is Dark Glasses?"

Henderson began denying everything. "Look, you've got this figured all wrong. Someone pulled a fast one on *all* of us. Yeah, some practical joker, maybe."

Slowly, Henderson began inching away. The brown paper bag was still tucked securely under his arm. Seizing his only chance for escape, he ran toward the open window and climbed onto the ledge outside. For a moment, everyone gasped, afraid he might fall. But he quickly inched his way out of view.

The children hurried after him, but it was too late. As Ben leaned outside, he could see that Henderson was already crawling along the ledge, heading for the window next door.

"After him!" shouted Mr. Reese, "before he gets away with a fortune."

Frantically, they all rushed toward the door.

But it was locked.

And the key was gone.

"It's too late," groaned Mr. Reese. "We'll never catch him now. Call the police. Call security. But I'm sure it's too late."

13

Katie was disgusted. "Ben, I told you to *hide* the key, not throw it out the window."

"Sorry," he said, sheepishly, "everything happened too fast. You were yelling, the flashbulbs were blinking and . . ."

"Never mind the explanation," argued Mr. Reese. "Make that call. And start banging on this door as hard as you can. Someone will surely hear us."

"Maybe one of us should climb out that window after him," suggested Ben, who felt responsible.

"Absolutely not," insisted Mr. Reese. "I won't

have you children endangering your lives because of that unscrupulous man."

Ben was relieved. He hated heights anyway.

The phone call seemed to produce little result. But after several minutes of pounding on the door and yelling frantically, they heard some noises outside in the hallway. Then they saw the lock slowly beginning to turn.

Two hotel security guards were standing outside.

So was the cabdriver, who'd been cheated out of his fare.

"There's been a robbery!" Katie shouted.

"You said it," the cab driver shouted back. "Yeah, fellas, these are the kids. Sure, I remember the short little one with the goofy Indian haircut. These punks stiffed me for three bucks on the meter. They ran out of my hack without paying."

"Three bucks? Who cares about that?" argued Hector. "We're chasing a *million*!"

Hartley Reese interceded. Taking out his wallet, he handed the cabby a twenty-dollar bill. "This should settle things."

The cab driver beamed. "Hey, thanks, mister."

"Think nothing of it," he said, about to rush out the door. "It's compliments of Melvin."

"I don't know who this Melvin guy is, but give him my regards."

"Darn," Hector groaned. "Henderson must've skipped by now."

"Maybe we can catch up with him in the lobby," suggested Katie.

"I wouldn't worry about that," said Detective McCullough, suddenly appearing in the doorway. "Henderson won't escape. I've posted police around the hotel. We got your message, but we didn't really need it. We were coming anyway."

"Thank goodness you got here," sighed Katie. "I was afraid you wouldn't come."

"When this cab driver called a while ago, I knew something must be up."

"Wow, this sure is fast service," said the cabby admiringly. "I take my hat off to you guys. Next time someone stiffs me, I'll know who to call." Tipping his cap, he left the room.

Shortly after, two policemen came rushing down the hall, with Victor Henderson in tow. Yelling and protesting, he still clutched the brown paper bag in his hand.

"I'll take that," said the detective. "It was mighty obliging of you to escape with the money, Henderson. If you hadn't, we might not have had a case."

The policemen dragged Henderson toward a chair, where they proceeded to clamp handcuffs on him.

Hartley Reese still couldn't believe it all. "Why did you do such a dreadful thing, Victor?"

"Oh, shut up. I was just protecting my investment."

"It beats me how you kids tied all this evidence together," said McCullough. "I didn't have any of it figured out until I checked up on that license plate number you gave me. After I tracked down that guy, things started making some sense."

"I knew it," squealed Hector. "Henderson had accomplices, right? That bum Barney Carter was in on the deal, too. And that sneaky guy in the dark glasses. Did you find out who he was?"

"We sure did. His name is Marvin Finkle. Of Finkle, Finkle, Finkle and Stern."

Ben was amazed. "Really? He looked too old to belong to a rock band!"

"Not a band, son," explained McCullough. "It's a law firm. Marvin Finkle was representing Barney Carter in his case against Victor

Henderson. He was planning to sue Henderson for a million dollars, plus a percentage of all Melvin's earnings. It seems Carter was telling the truth all along. Henderson *did* steal his cat."

Katie glanced at the disgruntled Henderson. "So that's why you did it. I knew how, but I couldn't figure out why."

"What choice did I have," shouted Henderson. "Carter slapped a law suit on me. I wish I *had* paid him that lousy ten bucks years ago. Then Melvin would've been mine, fair and square."

Katie pieced together the rest. "Instead, you thought you'd make a profit from the cat, even if you lost him in court."

"Sure. Even if the courts went against me, I'd still have a million bucks. I was gonna stash the dough in a safe deposit box. I knew Carter would be a likely suspect. With any luck, I'd get away with the dough, and he'd go to the clink."

"Well, if it hadn't been for these children," said Hartley Reese, "your plan might've worked."

"You're probably right," the detective agreed. "Though I'd begun doing a little checking on my own . . . unofficially, of course. It seems our Mr. Henderson has been involved in lots of phony deals: stock fraud and gambling, to name just two."

"No arrests, no convictions. And I'd have gotten away with this deal, too, if it wasn't for these lousy kids."

"And Omar's pendant," added Katie. "That's how I got my first clue. Melvin kept staring at it with his bright blue eyes. His eyes are what gave away his identity. Omar told me the pendant would bring good luck, and he was right."

Hector couldn't help feeling disappointed. "You mean Barney Carter had nothing to do with the catnapping?"

Katie laughed. "Face it, Hector. Carter just happens to be a lousy barber. He can't go to jail for that."

"On behalf of my company," said Mr. Reese, "please let me thank you children. If there's anything I can do to show my gratitude . . ."

"There is something," said Hector. "This investigation cost me money. I had eight dollars when I left home. Now I've got nothing."

"By all means, let me reimburse you." Hartley Reese took another twenty-dollar bill from his pocket and handed it to Hector. "Will this be sufficient?"

"Well, at least it'll pay for a decent haircut!"

14

The Camelot Hotel had never seen so much excitement. Before long, the lobby was crowded with policemen, reporters and several executives from Meow Chow, not to mention all the guests who were cat lovers, anxious to get a glimpse of Melvin.

Once all the confusion had died down, Detective McCullough personally escorted Katie, Ben and Hector home.

The children had so much to tell their parents, it was long after bedtime before the whole story had been unraveled.

"I still say we deserved some reward," Hector grumbled.

Katie and Ben glared at him as the telephone rang.

"I'm surprised at you, son," said Mr. Morrison. "Haven't we taught you that good deeds are their own reward? You'll have to settle for that."

"Perhaps you'll have to settle for fame," said his mother, hanging up the phone. "Channel Six would like you children in the studio tomorrow morning. You're going to be interviewed on television."

Hector beamed. "Yippee! Free advertising!"

"What's that mean?" asked his father.

"Wait and see," groaned Katie.

The next morning, the children arrived at the TV studio, accompanied by their parents. They were almost late. Hector had insisted on getting a decent haircut before he appeared before the world.

The newsman, Walter Whitner, greeted them warmly.

"Folks, this is Katie and Hector Morrison and Ben Colby. Sit down kids, over there next to Mr. Reese. Now tell our TV viewers how you happened to crack this case."

Hector stared at himself in the monitor, then smiled into the camera. "*I* gave my sister the first clue. You see, I know all there is to know about cats. In fact, I have my very own cat-sitting service. If any of you folks out there in TV Land want someone to take care of your darling kitties, I'm your man."

"Very interesting. And now, ladies and gentlemen, I'd like to introduce you to Hartley Reese, the president of Meow Chow. I'm sure all our viewers are waiting to be reassured that Melvin is alive and well."

Mr. Reese opened the carrying case beside him and lifted out Melvin. "As you can see, he's safe and sound."

The cat was his old self again: clean, white, bright-eyed and ready to perform. As the camera zoomed in on him, he opened his mouth and meowed as if on cue.

Mr. Reese beamed with pleasure. "Yes, indeed, Melvin is in top form and ready to go back into the studio. At the moment, he is in my custody, until the courts decide his legal ownership. Since I'm a cat lover myself, Melvin will have a safe, happy, temporary home with me. Melvin would also like to thank all his fans out there for the mail that poured into my office this weekend. Everyone was wishing him well and hoping for his safe return."

"I understand Melvin has just signed a new contract," said Mr. Whitner. "Can you tell us something about that, Mr. Reese?"

"Gladly. Just this morning, Melvin paw-graphed his new contract with Odyssey Pictures. He'll be making a movie in London this summer. Very soon, his fans will be able to see him on movie screens all across the country. And I'd personally like to use this opportunity to invite the Morrison and Colby families to join Melvin in England this July. Of course, all their expenses will be paid by Meow Chow."

The children could hardly believe their ears.

"That's wonderful," shouted Katie.

"Terrific," said Ben.

"*All* expenses?" asked Hector.

"Yes, air fare and hotel accommodations for two weeks. I'd also like to present each of you children with the new Melvin video game, which will be on sale in all toy stores this Christmas."

Katie felt as if she were on a game show, not a news program. "How can we thank you, Mr. Reese?"

"You already have. For rescuing Melvin, you deserve even more."

"*Is* there more?" asked Hector, hopefully.

"As a matter of fact, there is. But first, I'd like you children to tell the audience all about your special club."

"Well," said Katie, "we call it R.I.S.K. That stands for Rescuers In Search of Kitties."

"*I* thought up the name," interrupted Hector.

Ben continued. "We pick up strays in the street and find them good homes."

"Very commendable," said Mr. Whitner.

Hartley Reese agreed. "You know, Melvin was once a stray himself. Because of that, in Melvin's name, my company would like you children to have a lifetime supply of Meow Chow for your orphans."

Katie was thrilled. "Thanks a million."

Ben was, too. "What a great gift."

Hector admired Mr. Reese's business sense. "Say, that's great public relations. I bet you sell a mess more Meow Chow."

Hartley Reese blushed.

"Yeah, I know lots about advertising," Hector continued. "Businessmen have to. Did I tell you about *my* business? I have a cat-sitting service. If any of you folks out there . . ."

"I'm afraid we're out of time," interrupted Mr. Whitner. "So, let me thank you all for coming down to the studio today. America can now rest easy, knowing that the members of R.I.S.K. have rescued the most famous cat in the country!"